MARC BROWN

ARTHUR TRICKS THE TOOTH FAIRY

Step into Reading® Sticker Books

Random House 🏠 New York

Text and illustrations copyright © 1997 by Marc Brown. All rights reserved under International and Pan-American Copyright Conventions. Published in the United States by Random House, Inc., New York, and simultaneously in Canada by Random House of Canada Limited, Toronto.

http://www.randomhouse.com/

Library of Congress Cataloging-in-Publication Data:
Brown, Marc Tolon. Arthur tricks the tooth fairy / by Marc Brown. p. cm.
"Step into reading sticker books." SUMMARY: Jealous when Arthur loses a tooth and receives a dollar for it, his sister tries to trick the Tooth Fairy into also visiting her.
ISBN 0-679-88464-5 (trade). — ISBN 0-679-98464-X (lib. bdg.)
[1. Tooth Fairy—Fiction. 2. Teeth—Fiction. 3. Animals—Fiction. 4. Brothers and sisters—Fiction.]
I. Title. PZ7.B81618Alg 1998 [E]—dc21 97-25787

Printed in the United States of America 10 9 8 7 6 5 4 3 2 1

STEP INTO READING is a registered trademark of Random House, Inc.

Arthur ran to the breakfast table.

"Look, D.W.," he said.

Arthur waved a dollar.

"The Tooth Fairy left it

under my pillow."

"Why?" asked D.W.
"She takes baby teeth
and leaves money,"
Arthur said.

"That's goofy," said D.W.

"What does she do

with all those old teeth?"

Arthur thought

"Maybe her castle is made

of teeth," he said.

"Where does she get the money?"

asked D.W.

"You ask too many questions,"

said Arthur.

The next morning

D.W. ran to the breakfast table.

"My tooth is loose!" she shouted.

"It is not," Arthur said.

"Is too," said D.W.

"Nope. You are too young
to lose teeth," said Arthur.

"Not fair!" said D.W.

When Arthur got home from school,
the house was very noisy.
Slam! SLAM! **SLAM!**
went D.W.'s door.
"What are you doing?"
shouted Arthur.
"Pulling out my loose tooth,"
said D.W.
"Oh, no! Stop it!" said Arthur.
"Your tooth is NOT loose."

That night D.W. said,

"I have a toothache.

My tooth needs to be pulled out."

"Mom, she's making it up,"

said Arthur.

"Am not," said D.W.

"It really hurts."

"If it still hurts tomorrow,
we'll visit the dentist
on our way to the museum,"
said their mother.

The next day they went
to the dentist.
D.W. jumped into his chair.
"Your teeth are perfect,"
said the dentist. "I don't think
the Tooth Fairy will visit you
for a year or two."
"See, I told you," said Arthur.
"No one believes me," cried D.W.

STERILIZER

COTTON

My Own Arthur Story

by ....

Can you write and illustrate
a story about Arthur, D.W.,
and their friend Francine
having fun on a snowy day?
Here are some stickers
to get you started.
Have fun!

D.W. dragged her feet
all the way to the museum.
Everywhere she looked
she saw teeth.
Dinosaur teeth.

Shark teeth.

 Tiger teeth.

D.W. could not stop thinking
about teeth.

At the museum shop
their mother said,
"You can each buy
one little thing."
Arthur looked
at everything.

But D.W. knew just what
she wanted.
"I'm going to buy
a shark's tooth," she said.
"I have a great idea!"

That night D.W. couldn't wait
to go to bed.
"I'll tell you a secret, Arthur,
if you promise not to tell
Mom and Dad," said D.W.
"Promise," said Arthur.
"The Tooth Fairy
is coming tonight.
I'm going to trick her
with my shark's tooth,"
said D.W.
"It's really going to work."
"I sure hope so," said Arthur.
"Because I'm tired of hearing
about teeth."

That night D.W. dreamed
about the Tooth Fairy.

And that night Arthur decided
that the Tooth Fairy
needed a little help.

he sun was up,

ran into Arthur's room.

k! Look what the Tooth Fairy

left me!" she shouted.

Arthur opened his eyes.

"I tricked the Tooth Fairy!
I tricked the Tooth Fairy!"
sang D.W.
"I did it. I really did!"

"And tonight I'm going
to do it again!" shouted D.W.